This annual belongs to:

....

....

HiT entertainment

Thomas the Tank Engine & Friends™

Britt

Based on the Railway Series by the Reverend W Awdry
© 2009 Gullane (Thomas) LLC. A HiT Entertainment company
Thomas the Tank Engine & Friends and Thomas & Friends are trademarks of Gullane (Thomas) Limited.
Thomas the Tank Engine & Friends and Design is Reg. U.S. Pat. & Tm. Off.

EGMONT
We bring stories to life

First published in Great Britain in 2009 by Egmont UK Limited
239 Kensington High Street, London W8 6SA

Editor: Nina Filipek
Designer: Dan Green

ISBN 978 1 4052 4635 4

10 9 8 7 6 5 4 3 2 1

Printed in Italy

THOMAS & FRIENDS™

· Annual 2010 ·

Contents

"Hello, I'm Thomas!
I'm a Really Useful Engine and so are all
my friends. You can read about our
adventures in this special annual."

Thomas' Alphabet

A a

Arthur is the largest tank engine on Sodor.

B b

Bertie is a friendly little bus.

C c

Colin is a cheerful, canal-side crane.

D d

Duncan thinks he knows best!

E e

Emily is a clever bossy buffers!

F f

Flora is a new steam tram.

G g

Gordon is the fastest engine on Sodor!

H h

Hank is a big, new steam engine.

Island of Sodor, where Thomas and his friends live.

I i

J j

James is the only red engine.

Knapford Station is the biggest station on Sodor.

K k

L l

Lady Hatt is The Fat Controller's wife.

 **Murdoch** can pull very heavy loads. **M m**

N n **Neville** is everyone's friend!

 **Oliver** was rescued from the scrapyard! **O o**

P p **Percy** likes to take the mail.

 The engines collect slate and stone from the **Quarry**.

Rosie has purple paintwork!

R r

S s

Spencer is silver-coloured and very fast.

Thomas is a cheeky little tank engine!

T t

U u

Edward goes **under** the bridge.

The engines go over the **Viaduct**.

V v

W w

This **whistle** belongs to a Guard.

X x

X looks like the sails on the windmill.

Y y

Molly is a bright **yellow** engine.

Z z

Bertie is taking his passengers to the **zoo**.

Spot the Difference

Here comes Thomas with Hank, the new steam engine. Hank has made lots of friends on Sodor and he's already a Really Useful Engine!

These two pictures of Thomas and Hank look the same, but there are 5 things that are different in picture 2. Circle the differences and tick the box as you find each one.

1 ☐ 2 ☐ 3 ☐ 4 ☐ 5 ☐

Thomas in Trouble

One day, Thomas and Emily were in for repairs at the Fitter's Yard.

Soon, Emily was ready to go back to work but Thomas had to wait for his final inspection.

He was still waiting when James puffed in to the Yard to deliver some paint. **"Bust my boiler!"** James laughed. "You've broken down, Thomas!"

"No, I haven't!" huffed Thomas, crossly.

"You must have done," snorted James. "Otherwise you wouldn't be at the Fitter's Yard."

Just then, The Fat Controller arrived. "Thomas!" he boomed. "Are you ready to take the School Choir to their concert?"

"Nearly ready, Sir," puffed Thomas, excitedly.
"Nearly ready isn't good enough!" The Fat Controller replied.
Thomas didn't want anyone else to collect the Choir so he decided to leave before his final inspection.
"I'm ready now, Sir!" he puffed, and headed off to pick up his carriages, Annie and Clarabel.

Further down the line, Thomas began to make strange noises.

"Clangety-clong, something's wrong!" sang Annie and Clarabel.

But Thomas wasn't listening and soon he arrived at Knapford Station.

"Who's making that nasty noise?" wheeshed Emily. "Did you have your final inspection, Thomas?"

"I'm fine!" Thomas huffed.

The Choir got on board and he steamed away,
"Clangety-clong, clangety-clong!"

Thomas was feeling hot and bothered when he had to stop at a signal.

Toby saw that something was wrong. "Did you take on enough water at the Fitter's Yard?" he asked.

"There's nothing wrong with me!" replied Thomas, crossly.

When Percy saw Thomas at a level crossing, he was rattling and steaming more and more. "What's happened to you?" cried Percy.

But Thomas didn't like being told there was something wrong with him, so when the barrier opened he huffed away.

Then there was trouble! Thomas began to chuff slower and slower. Steam burst from his boiler and black smoke flew from his funnel. He had broken down!

The Choir began to sing while they waited.

"The children will be late for their concert and it's all my fault," he wailed, sadly. **"I've let everyone down."**

Just then, Gordon came around the bend. He could see that Thomas was in trouble but he couldn't stop to help because he had his own passengers on board.

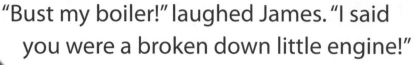

Then, Thomas heard a whistle. It was James! Thomas tooted as loudly as he could. **"Stop!"**

"Bust my boiler!" laughed James. "I said you were a broken down little engine!"

"I am," sighed Thomas. "And I need your help. Can you take the Choir to their concert?"

James was happy to help his friend. **"I'll get them there on time!"** he wheeshed.

Now Thomas knew he had to go back to be repaired as quickly as possible.

Henry was sent to collect Thomas and shunt him to the Fitter's Yard.

Before long, Thomas was as good as new! **And this time he waited for his final inspection!**

"You have been very patient, Thomas," said The Fat Controller. "I have a special job for you. You are to collect the Choir and bring them home again."

"Thank you, Sir!" tooted Thomas.

Thomas chuffed to the concert, smiling all the way, **"Clangety-clong, nothing is wrong!"** he laughed.

Follow the Tracks

Show Thomas and Emily the way to the Fitter's Yard by following the railway tracks.

Finish

Help Thomas find the right track from the Fitter's Yard to Knapford Station, picking up Annie and Clarabel on the way.

Finish

Duncan Does It All

Duncan was feeling fed up when he arrived at the Wharf one afternoon.

"What's the matter?" tooted Thomas.

"I've been doing the same job all day," grumbled Duncan. "Collecting silly straw and taking it up to the farms."

Just then, Rusty puffed in, looking tired. "Hello," he wheeshed. "I have so many jobs to do today. I'm out of puff already!"

"What sort of jobs?" asked Duncan.

"I have to pick up some passengers and show them the Ruined Castle," chuffed Rusty.

Duncan thought that sounded more exciting than delivering straw. "I'll pick up your passengers for you," he tooted, eagerly.

So Duncan left his trucks of straw and was soon chuffing cheerfully through the beautiful countryside.

"Look at the sights, look at the sights!" his wheels clickety-clacked along the tracks.

He was enjoying his new job!

When he arrived at the Castle, the people got out to take some photographs. But Duncan didn't like waiting and wished he had something else to do.

Just then, Skarloey puffed up.

"Flatten my funnel!" he whooshed. "These trucks are heavy. I hope I'm not too late for my next job."

"What is your next job?" Duncan asked.

"I have to collect sheep from the farm," said Skarloey, "and take them to market."

Duncan thought that sounded exciting so he told Skarloey that he would collect the sheep and take them to market. The people at the Castle were very surprised when Duncan puffed off without them!

Duncan soon arrived at the farm. He coupled up to the sheep trucks and trundled off to market. **"This is much more exciting than pulling passengers,"** he tooted.

Further up the track, he saw Sir Handel at the water tower. "What are you doing today?" asked Duncan.

"A very special job," wheeshed Sir Handel, grandly. "I have to collect a merry-go-round from the Transfer Yards."

Duncan thought that sounded really exciting. His boiler bubbled!

"I'll do it for you!" he wheeshed.

And, before Sir Handel could say anything, Duncan raced away to the Transfer Yards!

Duncan was feeling pleased with himself. He'd had such an exciting day!

But then he saw The Thin Controller, who looked cross.

The Farmer had just been on the telephone.

"His straw hasn't been delivered, there are people in his field and his sheep haven't arrived at market!" said The Thin Controller, sternly.

"Bust my buffers! It's all my fault, Sir," sniffed Duncan. "I asked Rusty and Skarloey if I could do their jobs, but I didn't finish them properly."

"You haven't done your own job either, Duncan," said The Thin Controller, sharply.

Duncan knew The Thin Controller was right and he promised to go back and deliver the straw straight away.

Duncan was by the lake when he saw Rusty.

"Do you want to help take my passengers to the forest?" tooted Rusty.

"No, thank you," chuffed Duncan.

Then he saw Skarloey unloading the sheep. "Next, I have to collect some cows," he whistled. "Do you want to help?"

"No, thank you," chuffed Duncan. **"Delivering my straw is just as exciting."**

When Duncan finally arrived with the straw the Farmer was pleased to see him and that made Duncan feel happy. Now he had finished his job properly like a **Really Useful Engine!**

Duncan's Story Quiz

Now that you have read Duncan's story, see if you can answer the questions about it. Tick the right answers to the questions below.

1. Where was Duncan taking the straw?

the School

the Farm

Maithwaite Station

2. Who did Duncan take to the Ruined Castle?

the Stationmaster

the passengers

the Farmer

3. Which two engines did Duncan help in the story?

Skarloey

Rusty

Thomas

4. Who was supposed to collect the merry-go-round?

Sir Handel

Thomas

Emily

5. Who was cross with Duncan?

The Engineer

The Thin Controller

The Duke of Boxford

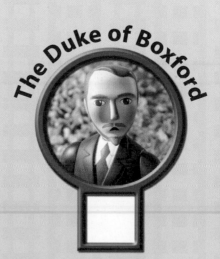

ANSWERS: 1. the Farm, 2. the passengers, 3. Skarloey and Rusty, 4. Sir Handel, 5. The Thin Controller.

31

Hide and Peep

One day, Thomas, Percy and Cranky were at Brendam Docks waiting for an important cargo ship to arrive.

Cranky could see that the ship was far away.

"Let's play a game while we wait," said Thomas. "You go and hide, Percy, and when I find you I will peep loudly!"

Hide and Peep was Thomas' favourite game!

Cranky, the tall crane, looked down at the little engines. **"Can I play?"** he asked.

"You're much too tall to hide!" laughed Thomas.

Cranky felt a bit left out when Thomas steamed off to find his friend.

Thomas puffed past platforms ... steamed by sidings ... and wheeshed alongside warehouses.

But Percy was good at hiding and Thomas couldn't find him anywhere. So Thomas decided to play a trick!

"Found you!" peeped Thomas, pretending he knew where Percy was hiding.

Percy puffed out of his hiding place but he could see that Thomas hadn't really found him at all.

"You tricked me!" Percy tooted, crossly.

"I'm sorry!" wheeshed Thomas.

Percy chuffed away to hide again. Thomas couldn't find him anywhere! But Thomas had another idea.

"Percy!" tooted Thomas, loudly. "The Fat Controller is here!"

He wasn't really!

"Bust my boiler! Where is he, Thomas?" puffed Percy.

"Found you!" peeped Thomas, cheekily.

Percy saw that Thomas had tricked him again!

"I'm sorry," Thomas chuffed. "Hide again. This time I won't trick you!"

So Percy puffed away to hide again.

Thomas was looking for Percy when he found the Dock Manager!

The manager told him that he and Percy had to collect their deliveries.

"Percy! The ship has docked!" Thomas tooted.

Percy heard him but he thought it was another trick so he stayed hidden.

"Cinders and ashes!" cried Thomas. "Percy thinks I'm playing another trick!"

Thomas knew that Percy would be in trouble if he didn't collect his cargo trucks on time.

Thomas raced over to Cranky. He was too tall to be a good hider but he might be a good finder.

Thomas asked Cranky if he could see where little Percy was hiding.

Cranky looked easily over warehouses ... across platforms ... and down into sidings ... and there he saw Percy!

"I've found him!" cranked Cranky, proudly.

Thomas raced over. "Found you, Percy!" he peeped, loudly.

"Rattle my rods!" puffed Percy. "You are the best finder after all!"

"No, I'm not!" peeped Thomas, sadly. "I had to ask Cranky to find you."

"You tricked me again," huffed Percy.

Before Percy could get cross, Thomas told him about the waiting cargo trucks. Together, Percy and Thomas steamed back to the Docks.

They arrived just in time to take their deliveries and soon they were ready to leave. But first, Thomas wanted to thank his friend, Cranky.

"Thank you, Cranky!" chuffed Thomas, loudly. **"You are the Best Finder!"**

Cranky was very pleased.

"And, Percy," puffed Thomas, **"you are the Best Hider ever!"**

Who's Hiding?

The engines are playing Hide and Peep! Can you find them all? As you name each one, say, "PEEP! Found you!"

Murdoch

Henry

Thomas

James

3

4

Read a Story

Now you know what happened in the Hide and Peep story, you can read it yourself! The little pictures will help you. When you see the pictures of Thomas and his friends, say their names.

Thomas

Percy

Cranky

The Fat Controller

One morning, and were playing

Hide and Peep at the Docks. wanted to

play, but said, "You're much too tall to

hide!" Now was very good at hiding.

 couldn't find him anywhere so he

decided to play a trick. "Found you!" tooted

 , pretending he'd seen .

"You tricked me!" peeped , crossly.

"I'm sorry. Hide again!" said  .

 went away to hide.

"Quick, is here!" said .

But it was another trick! was really cross.

"Hide again!" said . So went to

hide. Then tooted loudly, " , the

ship has docked!" stayed hidden.

He didn't know that this time it wasn't a trick.

But  and would be in trouble if

they didn't collect their deliveries on time.

 asked if he could help. And, in no

time at all, shouted, "I've found him!"

"Thank you, !" chuffed . "You are

the Best Finder! And ... , you are the Best

Hider ever!"

Gordon and the Engineer

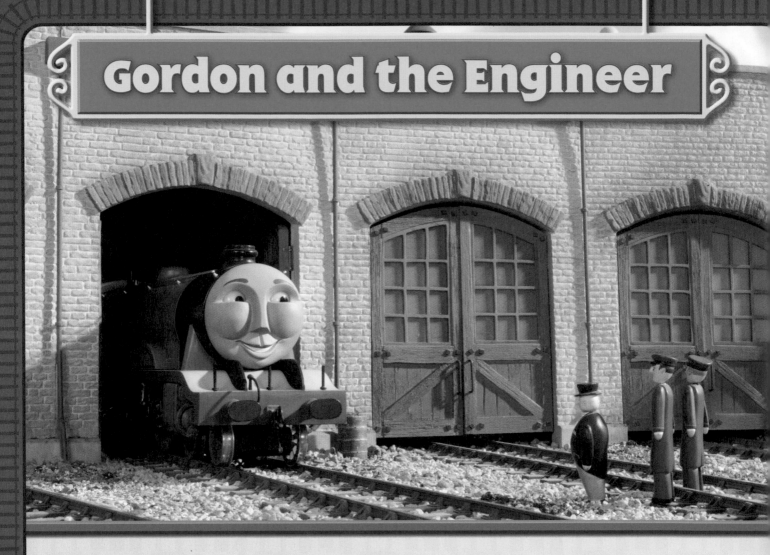

All the engines on Sodor have their favourite jobs. Gordon loves pulling the Express. He thinks it's the most important job on the Island!

One morning, The Fat Controller told Gordon that the points on the track were broken! Gordon had to collect an Important Engineer at Maron Station and take him to fix the points as quickly as possible.

So Gordon steamed off to Maron. **"I'm an Important Engine, collecting an Important Passenger!"** he chuffed, proudly.

All the other engines were stuck and couldn't go anywhere until the points were fixed.

Gordon pulled into Maron station. There was a passenger carrying a toolbox waiting on the platform. Gordon thought he must be the Important Engineer.

"All aboard!" whistled Gordon. The man with the toolbox climbed on board.

"Wait!" said the Stationmaster. "Bertie the Bus is bringing more passengers!"

Gordon told him he couldn't wait.

"I have a Very Important Passenger on board. I have to leave now!" And he left.

Gordon didn't know that the man with the toolbox wasn't the Engineer! Bertie the Bus had brought the Engineer with the other passengers.

Gordon rattled past Donald ... then clattered past Douglas.

"Important Engine coming through!" chuffed Gordon.

The man with the toolbox was pleased. He was the only passenger and he didn't have to stop at any of the stations.

Soon Gordon arrived at the broken points.

"I'm glad you're here!" puffed Thomas, and he told the man about the problem with the points.

"I'm not an engineer!" said the man with the toolbox.

Gordon realised his mistake – he'd picked up the wrong passenger! He told the Signalman that he was going back to get the Engineer.

"But you can't reverse down the Express line," said the Signalman.

"Maybe you could go on my line," said Thomas, helpfully.

So, leaving his coaches, Gordon steamed on to Thomas' track and reversed quickly down the line.

But he found Douglas blocking his path. "Out of my way!" huffed Gordon. "I've got an Important Passenger to collect."

"You can't get past!" puffed Douglas. "I can only go back as far as the next station, then Donald is in the way!"

Gordon felt terrible.

All the engines were stuck – and it was his fault.

Then he had an idea. "Maybe all the engines can help," he thought.

He told Douglas his idea. Douglas puffed down the track to tell Donald.

And Donald puffed back to collect the Engineer!

The Engineer climbed on board ... then Donald chuffed back up the line and dropped him off at the station.

Then Douglas took the Engineer to the next stop where Gordon was waiting for him.

It was a grand plan and it worked!

Finally, Gordon took the Engineer to the broken points. The points were soon fixed and the engines could chuff through.

"Thank you, Gordon!" tooted Thomas, happily.

Later that evening, the railway was back to normal.

"Thank you for helping me today," chuffed Gordon. **"Even an Important Engine like me needs help sometimes!"**

Find Four

Gordon's number is four. It's his favourite number in all the world!

Help Gordon to count four flags.

1 2 3 4

Tick the box if you can count four things the same in each row.

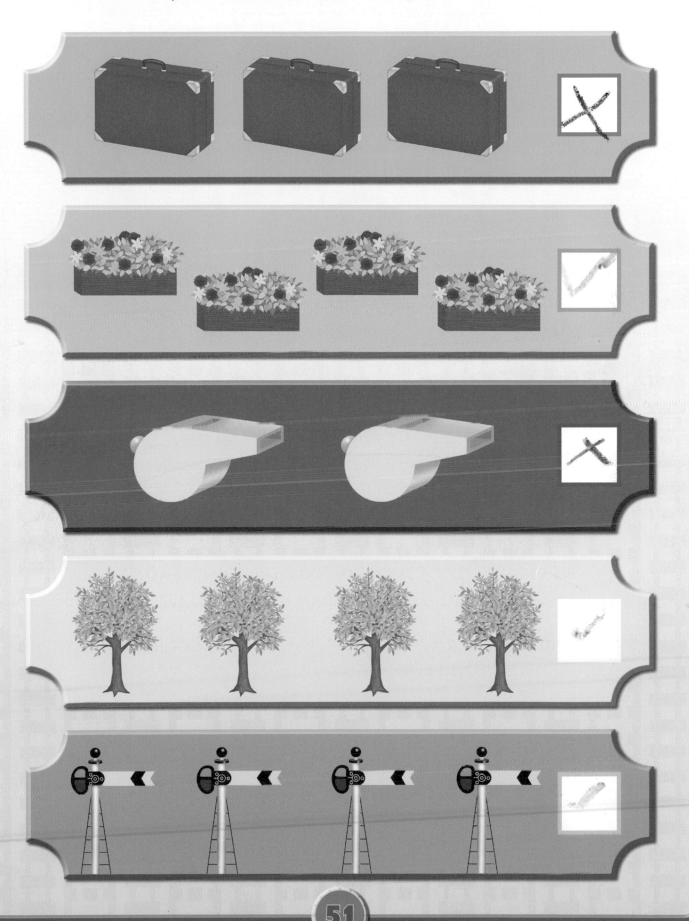

Dream On

One day Thomas was shunting trucks at Knapford Yards when The Fat Controller arrived.

"The Duke and Duchess of Boxford are coming to Sodor with Spencer," he said. "Spencer will be very tired after his long journey. So you, Thomas, must help him."

Spencer was a special engine from the Mainland and he was a bit of a show-off.

Later that day, Spencer arrived. **"Take my carriages and shunt them away!"** Spencer huffed at Thomas.

Spencer didn't like having to wait while Thomas finished another job.

"I'm faster, shinier and stronger than you, Thomas. You are just a little tank engine!" he sniffed.

Thomas felt cross but he kept his promise and shunted Spencer's carriages safely into the sheds.

Thomas was very tired when he got back.

"Anyone can shunt trucks," Spencer told Thomas. "But you have to be Very Special to pull the Duke and Duchess of Boxford."

This made Thomas cross.

"I'll show that Bossy Boiler!" puffed Thomas to Percy. "Tomorrow I'm going to be faster, shinier and stronger than Spencer!"

The next morning, when Thomas reached the mainline, he puffed faster and faster. Faster than he'd ever puffed before!

He steamed past Emily. "Slow down, Thomas!" she whistled. "You'll never get round the bend!"

Thomas slammed on his brakes. "Woah!" tooted Thomas, scared. Luckily, he stopped just in time.

"Maybe I can't be faster than Spencer," he thought. **"But I can still be shinier and stronger!"**

Later, Thomas was at the wash-down.
"I'd like the shiniest polish ever!" he tooted.

Thomas was rubbed and scrubbed until he sparkled and shone!

Then Toby pulled up next to him with an important message. "You have to shunt stone at the Quarry," he steamed. "They are waiting for you now."

Thomas quickly made his way there. He felt proud when one of the other engines said, "You're the shiniest engine I've ever seen!"

But soon his trucks were filled with stone. He was dusty and dirty. All his sparkle and shine had gone.

As Thomas came to Gordon's Hill, he thought, **"I may not be faster or shinier than Spencer, but I can still be stronger."**

Then the hill got steeper, the stone felt heavier and his wheels started to spin.

"Oh, no!" cried Thomas, as he slid all the way to the bottom. **Now he felt very silly.**

After Thomas' wash-down the next morning, The Fat Controller told him that the Duke of Boxford had to return to the Mainland on Very Important Business.

"Where are Spencer's carriages?" he boomed.

"They're at the Yard, Sir," said Thomas. "I'll shunt them over to Spencer straight away!"

When Thomas arrived with the carriages, Spencer's boiler was still cold. "You might be the fastest, shiniest and strongest engine, but you're the slowest to get fired-up!" tooted Thomas, cheekily.

Then the Duke arrived and saw that Spencer wasn't ready. **"Thomas, you must take me to the Airport!"** he said.

"Yes, Sir!" tooted Thomas.

Thomas steamed proudly away, with the Duke's special badge gleaming on his boiler. He arrived just in time for the Duke's flight!

Thomas knew he wasn't faster, shinier or stronger than Spencer – but he was Reliable. **And that was a Really Useful thing to be!**

Look Closely

Thomas took the Duke of Boxford to the Airport.
He had the Duke's special badge on his boiler.

These close-ups can all be found in the big picture.
Tick the boxes when you have found them.

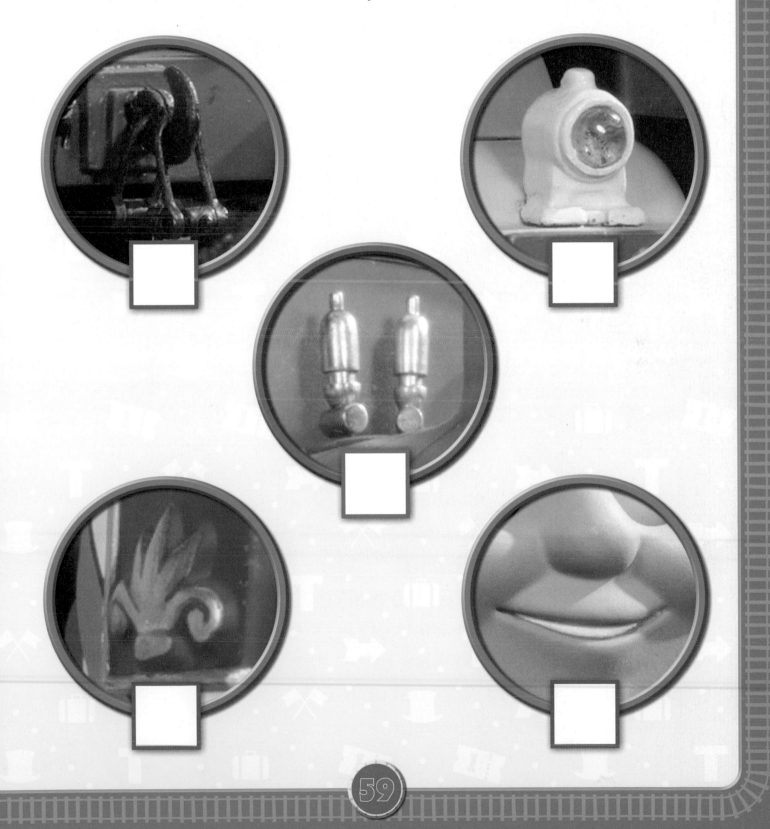

Edward and the Mail

Early one morning, The Fat Controller came to Tidmouth Sheds.

"Percy has broken down. He's at the Repair Yard," he told the engines. "I need another engine to take the mail."

"Edward could do it!" peeped Emily.

"Yes," huffed Henry. **"Edward knows how to do everything!"**

Edward had never taken the mail before and wanted to ask lots of questions. But he didn't want to look silly. "I'll have to work out how to do it by myself," he thought.

When Edward arrived at the mail depot, the Stationmaster was waiting.

"You have lots of parcels to deliver today," he said. "Some for Farmer McColl, some for the children's party at Maithwaite and some for the school."

Edward didn't know which of the parcels to deliver first.

He saw Thomas at the junction and thought about asking him, but Edward didn't want to look silly. So he made up his mind to take the parcels to the children's party first.

But he accidentally left Farmer McColl's parcels with the children, too!

Next, he delivered some parcels to the school ... and, finally, he delivered the rest of the parcels to Farmer McColl. **"That was easy!"** chuffed Edward. "I made all the deliveries and I didn't have to ask anyone how to do it!" He felt very proud.

But The Fat Controller was getting lots of phone calls. Edward had delivered the wrong parcels to the wrong places!

Poor Edward. He was upset when he found out what he'd done.

He knew he'd have to deliver the parcels again because everyone was waiting for them. He had to hurry!

First, he collected the parcels from the children's party. Then, he collected the parcels from the school.

"Now I have to collect the parcels from Farmer McColl!" puffed Edward. He steamed on. **"I mustn't be late, I mustn't be late!"**

Edward came to a junction. He didn't know which way was the fastest track to the farm and he didn't ask the Signalman.

"Stop!" shouted the Signalman. "That track is closed!"

Edward rattled around the bend and straight into a barrier – parcels flew everywhere!

"I'll never deliver the parcels on time now!"
he wheeshed.

Edward felt awful!

Soon the parcels were loaded back into Edward's trucks and he knew now he had to ask for help.

He steamed off to the Repair Yard. He was going to find Percy and ask him what to do.

Percy was still being fixed. He didn't think Edward was silly for asking at all.

"I deliver the parcels in a special order. I always start with the delivery that is furthest away," puffed Percy. "Then I work my way back to Tidmouth Sheds."

Edward felt happy as he chuffed away because now he knew exactly what to do.

The children got their parcels in time for the party. The right parcels were delivered to the school. And Farmer McColl was pleased to get his parcels, too.

Everyone was happy!

Edward had always been a clever engine. But now Edward felt cleverer than ever!

Parcel Puzzles

Now you have read the story, you can count how many parcels Edward delivered to each place. Then write the answers to the questions in the boxes below.

The Farm

The Party

The School

How many parcels for Farmer McColl?

How many parcels at the party?

How many yellow parcels can you spot?

Two the Same

Find two pictures of Edward that look exactly the same.
Circle the letters when you have found them.

Colour Percy

Colour in the picture of Percy using the little picture to help you.

See you next year!